WHAT TO DO

Pablo Katchadjian

WHAT TO DO

Translated from Spanish
by Priscilla Posada

DALKEY ARCHIVE PRESS

Originally published in Spanish as *Qué hacer*
by Bajo La Luna in 2010.
©2010 by Pablo Katchadjian
Translation copyright ©2015 by Priscilla Posada
First edition, 2016
All rights reserved

Library of Congress Cataloging-in-Publication Data
Identifiers: ISBN 9781564787057
LC record available at https://catalog.loc.gov/

Partially funded by a grant by the Illinois Arts Council

Dalkey Archive Press publications are, in part, made possible through the support of the University of Houston-
Victoria and its program in creative writing, publishing,
and translation.

Dalkey Archive Press
Victoria, TX / McLean / Dublin
www.dalkeyarchive.com

Cover: Art by Katherine O'Shea

Printed on permanent / durable acid-free paper

WHAT TO DO

Alberto and I are giving a lecture at an English university when a student, in an aggressive tone, asks: "When philosophers speak, is what they say true or is it a *double*?" Alberto and I look at each other, somewhat anxious for not having understood the question. Alberto reacts first; he steps forward and responds that it's impossible to know. The student, dissatisfied with this response, stands up (he's eight feet tall), approaches Alberto, grabs him, and stuffs him into his mouth. But although this looks dangerous, not only do the students and I laugh, but Alberto, with half his body inside the student's mouth, also laughs and says: It's fine, it's fine. Then, Alberto and I are suddenly in a plaza. An old man is feeding a flock of pigeons. Alberto approaches the old man and I get a bad feeling and want to stop him, but for some reason I can't. Before Alberto reaches him, the old man somehow becomes a pigeon and tries to fly, but can't. Alberto splints his wings and tells him that he'll get better soon, that his problem is very normal. The old man looks happy. Then we're suddenly in a restroom in a nightclub. For some reason, we're in the women's restroom. Five very pretty, well-dressed girls enter, sweaty from dancing so much. Alberto, up to something, approaches one of them, who seems to be very drunk or on drugs, and throws himself on top of her; from what I can see, she lets him do what he wants, although it's not exactly clear what it is that he wants to do, because he only rubs himself against her as if his body itches; she responds in the same manner, and so it looks like they're mutually scratching themselves. The other four approach me and suddenly the five of us are doing something that doesn't make sense. It's as if the scene were censored. Then I notice that the girls are old women; simultaneously, I hear Alberto talking to the drunk girl about Léon Bloy. He tells her that he wanted to be a saint and suffered because he couldn't. He goes over the part where Véronique has all of her teeth pulled out and, although he remains still, it looks as if he wants to pull this girl's teeth out. I grab him by the hood of his jacket and drag him outside of the restroom. It seems like Alberto is made of rags, he's very light.

Alberto and I go to a toy store to pick out a gift for his nephew. Alberto grabs a broom and tells me: This is what I want. He buys it; when we go outside, it's pouring. We stay under the toy store's awning, but the space keeps filling up in a striking manner making us more and more uncomfortable. As if we were in a box, we're pushed upwards by people who keep accumulating underneath us. When we reach the top, right before falling, we're suddenly teaching in an English university. Alberto is explaining the meter of Lear's limericks and somehow manages to relate everything to Lawrence of Arabia. I interrupt him to explain what Graves had to say about Lear, but Alberto gives me a look and whispers in my ear: Don't brag, it's not necessary. For some reason, what he says doesn't bother me and I take it as sound advice that he can also apply to himself. A student stands up and asks why anarchists placed bombs in restaurants. Alberto begins to explain; meanwhile, the student grows taller until he reaches the ceiling. Alberto doesn't realize the danger we're in and, very focused, talks about Saint Isidore's *Etymologiae*. To avoid having the tall student stuff him into his mouth again, I grab Alberto by the hood of his jacket and take him out of there. Suddenly we're in a bank; Alberto wants to sell a broom (which isn't the same one he bought before although he thinks it is). We reach the counter and Alberto explains his problem to the teller. She's naked but Alberto doesn't seem to notice. I try pointing this out but he scowls while motioning with his hand. I don't know how the transaction turns out, but afterwards Alberto seems like he's made of rags. I try moving him but only succeed in making him blink.

Alberto and I are in some kind of empty lot. About ten English students arrive and take their places as if we were in a classroom. Now it looks like we're in a classroom in an English university. I'm explaining one of Boethius's ideas, but Alberto interrupts me. The students get angry at him because, so they say, they're interested in what I'm teaching. But Alberto keeps interrupting and when he gets some words in, half the students listen to him and the other half insist that I keep talking. The situation keeps worsening until we're suddenly in a shoe-repair shop. Alberto gives his black boots to the cobbler and asks him to replace the heel. The cobbler does it in ten seconds and brags about his agility, saying: Ten seconds! Ten seconds! Alberto puts his boots on, but one heel is four inches higher than the other one. I tell Alberto that he won't be able to walk like that, but he doesn't understand the problem. Alberto pays the cobbler and we leave. Suddenly we're in a wine cellar. I see that there are about eight hundred people drinking wine. Alberto and I serve ourselves a glass each. The wine tastes like an old rag and Alberto agrees but says it doesn't bother him. A television goes on and suddenly there's a well-dressed man explaining how they filter the wine using old rags. Alberto is standing on his highest heel forcing me to look up when I talk to him. Being in this position, combined with the smell of old rags, makes me vomit. People shout at me and, to avoid an ugly situation, Alberto grabs me by the hood of my jacket and takes me out to a black courtyard. I feel made of rags, I have neither weight nor gravity, but I can't stop vomiting; it feels like what I'm vomiting doesn't come from my body but rather is suddenly right in my mouth and then falls to the floor. This continues until I notice that the vomit, upon falling, or right before falling, transforms into water. The water floods the black courtyard and without realizing it, we reach a university and give a lecture on Latin and Modern Greek.

Suddenly Alberto is there, accompanied by three others. These people, he tells me, are our English students. I listen to them talk and something catches my attention; I realize that they're speaking in English but I'm understanding them in Spanish; then I find out that they're speaking in Portuguese, but I hear them speaking in English and find myself understanding them in Spanish. I ask Alberto if the same is happening to him but he scowls and motions for me to keep quiet. Angry, I grab him by the elbow and this enrages one of the students. When I look at the student, I notice he's ten feet tall. I realize then that we're simultaneously on a bridge and on a ship. And yet, it all feels very natural. I ask Alberto what he thinks of this and he responds that it's all very natural. In that moment, the ship (which is just a ship now) begins to sink, and Alberto tells me: This will sink. We get on a raft that Alberto had and along with us, four women also get on: one young, three old. The young one is pretty and she's naked; the old women are very ugly and they're also naked, but they don't interest us. The young one approaches Alberto and when he rejects her, I realize she's simultaneously young and old. This feels terrible, and luckily we're suddenly on a bridge (not the same one as before). There are three Spanish students and they ask if we know why Bloy suffered so much. Alberto and I talk simultaneously. This works out perfectly because not only do we understand each other and they understand us, but they're also getting double the information. Still, it doesn't make sense why we talk about Balzac instead of Bloy: I refer to *Cousin Pons* and Alberto to *A Woman of Thirty*. But Alberto hasn't read *A Woman of Thirty* and the students catch on and start getting restless. Perhaps because of this, one of them, who is eight feet tall, grabs Alberto and stuffs him into his mouth. Alberto doesn't seem surprised and says everything's fine. Regardless, I grab him by the hood of his jacket and take him out of the student's mouth. Alberto thanks me while wiping off the student's saliva, which he says will ruin his boots, with a rag.

I'm with Alberto and we're at an airport explaining a new relationship that we invented between John Donne and Lawrence of Arabia to an old woman. The old woman nods and asks: Would it be a mysterious relationship? The question throws us off, above all because we haven't fully read Donne—although we're experts on Lawrence of Arabia—and while we try responding, the old woman is suddenly not there and in her place there's a ten-foot-tall student. The background also changes and now we're in an English university. One of the students is a baby with a cow's head and Alberto makes me notice the medievalness of this image. I simultaneously believe and don't believe him, because I realize that, as much as the baby is medieval, all of that can't be medieval from any point of view. And yet, as if Alberto were granted his wish, everything becomes *distinctly* medieval. Now, it's a medieval airport and Alberto tells me: All of this is false. I respond yes, that the same happens with any dream. Alberto looks at me and says: No, no, I meant that *in any case* this is false. I try to pay attention but can't see anything clearly. Alberto points upwards. I see that there's someone watching and analyzing what we're doing. But we aren't doing anything, I tell him. This person notes everything down. Alberto tells him: To say something isn't to do something. This person above us keeps taking notes. We ask this person above us who he is, and he says, imitating the voice of an idiot, that he's an old rag. We ask him what he's doing and he tells us that we're his reality. We start laughing, partly because we're anxious and partly because his response is actually funny. To keep laughing, we ask him if he means to say that we're his or that he's for us; to our surprise, instead of responding, this person becomes the background and although we can see that the background is just an English university, we can't help but know that the background is a person, and that this person is an old rag, and yet the background isn't an old rag but rather the same English university. Despite all this, since we're in an English university, we try explaining the mysterious relationship between Donne and Lawrence of Arabia. We write on the blackboard: The seven pillars of Donne's wisdom. But, as we're beginning the lecture, the background envelopes us and takes us out of there as if we're made of old rags. In the darkness, I can notice Alberto blink.

I hear a noise and suddenly Alberto and I are in a room with four walls covered with shelves. The shelves are packed with small ceramic sculptures that lack a clear shape, or at least it's not clear to us. Alberto tells me: We're those sculptures. In that moment I see that the sculptures have my face *or* Alberto's, although I can't explain how they can have my face *or* his, that's to say, how something like this can also be undetermined. Suddenly I hear the noise from before, but stronger this time. Without knowing how, we're suddenly in another room, exactly like the one before, but now everything seems more unstable: the walls, the shelves, the sculptures. Even I, myself. I ask Alberto if he feels the same way, but he doesn't get to respond because the sculptures start falling from the trembling shelves. I panic and try to save them from destruction. But I can't and the sculptures fall, break into pieces, and all of this causes me much distress. That's when I see that Alberto has stopped trying to save the sculptures and that he's very calm, almost smiling. I shout at him to help me, but he says: It's better to throw everything before it falls on its own. I ask him to clarify what he means, but instead of responding he sweeps the sculptures off the shelves, destroying them, while shouting that it is. Seeing him so happy makes me want to imitate him and when I do, the joy I feel does me so much good that I can't help but break everything. I destroy the sculptures against the ceiling, against other sculptures, against themselves. We keep on like this, destroying everything we can, for a long time, and since there's always something just about to fall we keep on shouting happily, destroying ceramic sculptures.

I enter a house that looks like an English university and once inside I see Alberto. It seems to be eight or nine in the morning. Alberto and I move through the rooms and hallways until we reach a metal door; he opens it, we pass through, and then he closes it behind us. We see that we're in a courtyard and that we only have ten square feet of cement to stand on, because the rest is water, some sort of artificial lake. We try returning to the house but the door is locked. We don't know what to do and before we decide, ten students suddenly pass by on a raft and everything goes back to being an English university. We give a lecture. I want to talk about Stevenson, but Alberto wants to continue with Bloy. I suggest a middle ground, I tell him: Let's talk about Rubén Darío, about *The Odd Ones*. Alberto likes this idea and says that Darío hadn't read Lautréamont when he wrote about him, and that's why he relies on a review by Bloy. I tell him that he's breaching our agreement although I realize that what he's saying is true: that Bloy had written about Lautréamont, that Darío had read this review, and that he had stolen citations from it to use in his own work. But since we're arguing between us, instead of giving a lecture, the students, who are all eight feet tall, start getting angry. Since we know what could happen, we try to escape and suddenly we're running through a green and luminous meadow. We run so fast that we end up tripping and falling into a ditch of putrid water and old rag. I get out first and then pull Alberto up by the hood of his jacket. When he's finally out, I notice he's blinking.

Alberto and I are in a bar that resembles one from a foreign film (not English, but American). We call the waitress to order breakfast. When she leans over to clean the table, Alberto tries looking at her cleavage, and I copy him and do the same. We start asking for things in an attempt to see her cleavage: a coffee, a tea, to clean the table, croissants ... But I notice that as much as I try to look, I can't see anything because the view is blocked, that's to say, because there are holes in the depth of the dream that prevent us from seeing what would be there if the background were complete. I point this out to Alberto. The same is happening to him and after a confusing conversation, we discover that the background has these holes because it's made with an old rag. Suddenly, Alberto is a mummy. And even though the mummy's face isn't visible, I know the mummy is Alberto, for two main reasons: first, because his jacket's hood creates a bulge under the bandages; secondly, because the bandages are made of rags. We aren't in the bar anymore, but the waitress is with me and she's worried about Alberto's situation. I try looking at her cleavage although, in that moment, I'm certain that in reality she's an old woman and that looking at her cleavage is worthless. Instead, I try taking the bandages off Alberto, but as much as I try there are always more bandages. When I think I'm closer to his face, I see that it's not Alberto's face but rather that of a student from an English university, and I become very happy upon realizing that we're already in an English university and that Alberto is comparing Paul the Apostle to Paul the Anchorite while I explain Saint Isidore's "six ages of man." However, the students don't understand religion and accuse us of both being mystics and of bragging, and Alberto and I get a little anxious and start to blink. Then we hear a voice say: "So many other beautiful things that will be explained to me in paradise." Alberto thinks I'm the one who said this and accuses me of being pretentious. I get so anxious that I start salivating while the students throw rocks at me, and Alberto, sorry for having instigated all of this, protects me with the hood of his jacket and some very thin old muslin-like rags.

I'm with Alberto and our pockets are full of cold butter. It's so hot that we fear the butter will melt and ruin our clothes. We run along a path, past a meadow full of something resembling dried fruit, and enter a house in which an old woman lives. She points at me and Alberto says: Your head is getting bigger. I look at myself in a mirror and see that my head is getting bigger, but the sensation I get is that everything's shrinking except my head, which remains its normal size. Alberto hands me a pair of scissors and I try cutting my hair to keep my head from growing, but I can't do anything because everything keeps worsening and becoming more and more confusing. In that moment, I realize that the cause of all these problems is the old woman who keeps shouting and making us anxious. I tell Alberto to quiet her by stuffing her mouth with an old rag. Alberto can't find an old rag so instead he stuffs her mouth with old muslin, which he does find. The muslin works in such a way that instead of shouts, the old woman produces a beautiful melody that enchants the whole forest (in that moment, we're in a forest). We leave the old woman and find ourselves in an English university, this time as students. And yet, the professors are also us, and it's terrible hearing ourselves argue over Bloy. We realize that we're sick of ourselves (I of myself, Alberto of himself). The argument is interrupted when someone with a very strange face tells us that if we continue with our mouths shut, we won't be able to talk. But we're talking and our mouths aren't shut so we come to the conclusion that this person's comment is a trap: they want us to protest upon noticing the falseness of their observation. So, we decide not to protest and it's then that we realize that the trap was more complex: the act of not protesting makes us keep our mouths shut and when this person makes their observation again, we can no longer protest because it's true.

I'm furious and indignant because Alberto won't stop talking about Borges in front of our students at the English university, who are enraptured with all the talk of mirrors, labyrinths, and doubles. Alberto isn't into these subjects, but knows they're good for captivating English students. Not only am I annoyed that he's talking about these things, but also that I, despite being knowledgeable about this subject, can't do what Alberto does because I refuse to talk about these things. I try to interrupt him by talking about Bloy, but the students scowl, they motion with their hands, they throw old rags and rocks at me . . . I'm left covered in old rags and rocks and as I'm about to drown, I'm suddenly on a ship that looks like an English university. Alberto is talking to an old woman. I head towards them but I'm blocked by someone who for some reason I know is poor-in-spirit. I escape from him and while looking for Alberto, I find a tavern with eight hundred drinkers. They offer me a little but I say no because I know that the wine tastes like muslin. Alberto is seated and talking with the old woman. I approach them, but again I'm blocked by the poor-in-spirit and he starts crying while showing me a blank piece of paper.

I escape from him again and sit down with Alberto and the old woman who turns out to be a waitress. Alberto is talking to her about Borges and I get really mad because he could talk to her about something more interesting. I grab him by the hood of his jacket but he grabs me by mine and we end up crossed and completely immobilized. We suddenly find ourselves falling, in this same position, indefinitely. In the background, we hear an old woman singing some sort of music; due to this sensation, it feels like we're in paradise.

Alberto and I are in some type of entrance hall at an English university where there's a brain competition. What they do is weigh the participant's brains and the heaviest one wins something that is undefined (you can see it in a glass case but you can't make it out). Alberto and I compete and lose, although we thought we could win; suddenly, the poor-in-spirit shows up and wins, although everyone knows he's not intelligent. An argument breaks out when Alberto shows me that he no longer has teeth. I check and I'm also missing mine. When I look behind us, I see a group of people who I know are fascists, although nothing in their appearance indicates this. When I think I'm certain that they have our teeth, Alberto looks at me and I see that he's a mummy again. I worry and don't know what to do, but in that moment, with impressive clarity, the following logic presents itself to me:

– Alberto is a mummy
– Lenin was mummified
– Lenin wrote *What Is to Be Done?*
– Alberto will tell me what to do

I'm about to ask him but realize that I can't because the logic is written on a blackboard and we're in an English university giving a lecture on Ilya Kabakov's work, which according to Alberto can be related to *The Seven Pillars of Wisdom*, although I prefer to relate his work to Bloy's exegesis or Origen's voluntary castration (equally). None of the students understand these relationships and that's because they left their brains back at the competition and because we, more than lecturing, are bragging. So, we ask each other what to do, and Alberto, in contrast to what is written on the blackboard, doesn't know. In that moment we hear the song of the old woman with muslin in her mouth and suddenly we're in a forest whose trees look like they're made of old rags. We hear eight hundred wine drinkers in the background. The wine drinkers sing something that goes really well with the old woman's melody. The final feeling is that this moment is perfect, although we feel heavyhearted: it could be the lack of teeth or the lack of a brain.

I feel that my head is too heavy and Alberto tells me not to worry. But Alberto also feels really bad and we decide to go see a doctor. The doctor's office looks like a tavern and while we ask ourselves how this is possible, we notice something weird about the doctor. Alberto tells me: He's the poor-in-spirit. And then he tells me that the group of fascists and the poor-in-spirit are behind all of this. When I ask him what he means by "all of this," Alberto tells me: I'm referring to the disaster of all of this. I understand him perfectly and although it's clear that I understand, it's not exactly clear what it is that I understand. I'm trying to explain this to myself when an old woman approaches us, and her coming closer makes us happy and alleviates our worries. Right after, we notice that the old woman doesn't need a rational structure to understand us and that this is what does us so much good: we feel understood. But in that moment, I discover that the old woman is simultaneously the waitress; I ask Alberto if he notices this and he says yes. This cuts suddenly and now Alberto wants to give his nephew a broom he's holding. Then there's another cut and Alberto wants to take his black boots to the cobbler. I get anxious because I feel that Alberto is living these situations differently from me. I try to convince him that his boots are fine and that we're in danger, but Alberto doesn't notice anything: he keeps insisting with the broom and with his boots, but alternately, that's to say, he goes from one thing to the other though the two are unrelated between themselves: when he talks about the broom he forgets the boots and when he talks about the boots he forgets the broom. To save him, I grab him by the hood of his jacket and take him out of there. Then suddenly we're in a forest so clear that Alberto understands, by contrast, the danger we were in before. The contrast, on the other hand, makes me forget everything. We feel very light and think about Kovalevskaya's and Lenin's brains together, that's to say, mathematics and revolution; this is the subject that we explain when we're suddenly in an English university; the lecture begins with a quote from Simone Weil that Alberto writes on the board: "Unless one has exercised one's mind seriously at the gymnastic of mathematics one is incapable of precise thought, which amounts to saying that one is good for nothing."

We're in a classroom in an English university. Through
the window, I see that it's snowing and that it's possible
that the snow will bury us; to avoid thinking about this
danger and to prevent the students from noticing, I talk
about Saint Isidore while Alberto explains issues with the
translation of Saint Jerome's Bible. But suddenly, I want
to relate everything to Kropotkin's *The Conquest of Bread*
and this enrages Alberto; he tells me: We're already bragging. A student stands up and asks why the anarchists
placed bombs in restaurants. Alberto doesn't know what
to tell him and gets anxious. I grab him by the hood of his
jacket and suddenly we're in a restroom in a nightclub.
It's the women's restroom. It seems very calm and, in that
moment, we notice that the nightclub is empty because
it's three in the afternoon. Time passes very slowly until, just when we're about to get bored, we're suddenly in
the entrance hall of an English university. There are a lot
of people, and I get the feeling that they point at us and
make remarks. I ask Alberto and he says that he perceives
the same thing. I hear whispers behind us and realize that
those who are talking don't know that we can hear what
they're saying because what allows us to hear everything

is the acuity of our ears. Regrettably, we notice that our pockets are full of cold butter and we have to leave for fear of the heat. We look back and see that they're weighing the brains of five immigrants. They try to draw conclusions but they're arguing too much; finally, they start punching each other. In the distance, observing the fight and taking notes on everything, is the poor-in-spirit with two fascists. When we see them talk, we see that their teeth are blackened. We're talking about all of this when suddenly we're back in an English university; we dedicate the entire lecture to explaining that the only thing that distinguishes men from animals is that the former are reserved in showing their teeth. We explain: The instructions, for men, are to use their teeth but keep them hidden; in animals, to use and show them whenever necessary (in men it's never necessary to show them beyond what is expected by the rituals made to simultaneously confront and mock animals). We stop explaining because we notice that the students don't understand anything.

I'm with Alberto and we feel that our heads are shrinking; he asks me: What are we going to do with our hands when we no longer have heads? I respond, with difficulty because my jaw is tightening, that I don't know. In that moment we feel something like an equilibrium in the atmosphere, but still our heads keep shrinking. Alberto says: This is what I call balanced terror. He tells me it's thrilling, that's to say, that it's simultaneously good and bad. I correct him: You mean to say positive and negative. In response, he scowls and motions with his hand. Suddenly, the problem with our heads goes away and we're in a bank. Alberto wants to exchange the broom in his hand for a roll of dollars. The girl tells him he can't, but Alberto insists. In that moment, I look at the people in the bank. There are a few tourists, a poor-in-spirit, some old women, some immigrants, and some fascists. For some reason, I'm certain that some of them are terrorists. First I suspect the tourists; then the immigrants; then the old women; then the fascists; then the poor-in-spirit. But in that moment, I'm certain of one more thing: we ourselves are terrorists, although it's not because we *do* something terroristic, because neither we nor the others are doing anything. I ask Alberto if he feels like a terrorist and he tells me yes. I feel the same way. I ask the tourists and they tell me they do too; I ask the immigrants and they tell me that they think they do as well; I ask the old women and in response they show me the palms of their hands; the fascists don't answer and close their eyes and the poor-in-spirit tells me that he doesn't know and covers his ears. We're all afraid of ourselves. What could we come to do? We don't know and that's the problem: what would we be capable of? I ask Alberto what would we be capable of and he tells me that he doesn't know and that he also doesn't know what to do with his hands. We relax when we're suddenly in a plaza and there's an old man who is simultaneously a pigeon. His wings are broken and Alberto heals him with his hands. Alberto tells me: I use my hands for this. I lift my thumb to show approval, but Alberto doesn't notice because he's busy. When I decide to try and help him, the old man is already flying. The sky becomes very luminous and suddenly we're in an English university. I suggest we talk about the apocryphal correspondence between Seneca and Paul the Apostle, but Alberto, to avoid bragging, wants to talk about plumbing, about the principle of water valves. We come to an agreement and decide to analyze the apocryphal correspondence between Seneca and Paul the Apostle according to the logic of water valves. The students are very happy and applaud so much that they can't hear us.

Alberto and I are in an English university giving a lecture, but for some reason we can't bear the situation any longer and leave. There happens to be a bridge outside the classroom. It's very windy, so windy that my scarf blows away and Alberto loses the broom that he had in his hand and was planning on giving to his nephew. Regardless, we remain standing in the middle of the bridge as if we're waiting for something important. And a lot happens, but it's not clear what happens nor whether anything really happens. For example, I'm wearing my scarf again and Alberto has the broom back in his hand. So then: had these things really been lost? That, we cannot know. Suddenly we're in an English university explaining this, which Alberto decides to call a paradox, although I don't agree. But we can't finish the explanation because suddenly we're back on the bridge and our things blow away again, but this time, compared to last time, the fact that our things have blown away makes my heart feel heavy. I ask Alberto if the same thing is happening to him and he tells me yes. In that moment, we understand that we have had this weight even before we began to feel it and that this same weight is what made us unable to bear the English university any longer. But Alberto comes up with another solution: weigh the weight. We're talking about this when suddenly we're in an English university: of healing with that which is harmful; of poisoning poison; that's to say, of Hippocrates against Galen.

We're relating Juvenal and Persius to Bloy. The relationship is so obvious that the students in the English university don't understand it. One of them, who is eight feet
tall, asks in a threatening tone: Those contents are irrational? Neither Alberto nor I understand the question,
but from somewhere inside of me, a voice tells him yes,
that the contents are irrational because they emerge from
who knows where (or because it's not known from where
they emerge), but that the system of contents is the only
rational thing that exists and that we should trust in that.
The student, now with a double voice, asks: The system
is truly rational? We still don't understand the question,
but I answer him again in a voice that's as if it weren't
mine, or at least I feel that it's not mine: Yes, the system
is truly rational, but don't get confused: the idea of the
system is irrational and its origin is also irrational; what
is rational, truly rational, is its function and its logic.
The student agrees and leaves. Everyone follows him out.
Alberto and I are left sitting there, behind a desk, and
Alberto asks: From where did you pull all those stupid
things you said? I respond that I didn't say them, that
they came out of me like that from somewhere and that

the words themselves were irrational because, as much as they had their logic, we didn't know their origin. In that moment, on the ship (because now we know that we're on a ship and that we've always been on a ship: it's a certainty), we hear beautiful music coming from two places: from eight hundred wine drinkers and from one old woman. When we think about the drinkers, we're in a tavern; when we think about the old woman, we're in a forest: it all depends on where we place our attention. What we don't understand is how this is even possible if both types of music are emitted simultaneously, that's to say, if the music is a perfect blend of both places, of the forest and the tavern. When we understand this, we're suddenly explaining it in an English university: it was eight hundred old women producing this music. Alberto, to avoid enraging the students, tells them that it's all a poetic construction.

Alberto feels like getting up from the floor (he's on the floor) and I tell him that it won't be good for him. I'm also on the floor and try to get up, but can't. Then, we're suddenly in an English university and we teach. Then we run through a forest. Then we're in a tavern with eight hundred wine drinkers. Then in a plaza where there's an old man who is also a pigeon. Alberto tries fixing his broken wings but the old man takes off flying. Then we find out that his wings weren't broken, although watching him fly there are no doubts that his wings are completely broken and that with each beating of his wings another bone breaks. Nevertheless, the old man keeps flying just fine. As part of the background, as if coming from the sky, we hear an old woman singing music. The music moves us and makes us regret our situation.

We're in a classroom in an English university explaining a new relationship that we invented between Paul the Anchorite, Paul the Apostle, and Kleist. Alberto tries to show that the Marquise from *The Marquise of O . . .* was impregnated by a saint, and supports his argument with some apocryphal proverbs by Paul the Apostle. But soon I notice that my head is getting bigger and that I simultaneously have cold butter in my pockets. I begin to feel anxious and want to go outside to get fresh air, but the size of my head prevents me from passing through the door. For a moment, I'm inside and outside *simultaneously*; but this doesn't last long and next I'm only inside. Curiously, no one notices; afterwards I find out (from what they say) that to them my head is fine so they don't have anything to notice. But as much as they think that, in that moment, I'm certain that my head is increasing in size and know that this represents a danger to me and everyone else. I try discussing this with Alberto but he scowls and motions for me to keep quiet. Suddenly we're in a tavern and my head keeps growing. Alberto keeps not noticing, but the drinkers are very anxious because they know there's a latent danger. A couple of them go outside to vomit in a black courtyard. I take advantage of this moment of confusion to ask Alberto to take a good look at my head. We're in the middle of that when suddenly the focus shifts from my head to the smell of old rags. That's to say, that now no one, not even I, myself, thinks about the size of my head. The smell of old rags makes us nauseous, and everything continues in a state of seemingly endless nausea, like a continuous and suspended retching.

We're trying to make the students of an English university understand what Debord saw in Thucydides. The students understand it perfectly, but Alberto insists on repeating it over and over again. Each time he repeats it, the students come to understand him again. And everything seems to go on like this until one student, who is eight feet tall, grabs Alberto and stuffs him into his mouth while saying that our lecture is all "chicanery." He repeats "chicanery" so many times that the other students start saying the same thing. Without me realizing it, Alberto is suddenly not there: only a piece of his jacket's hood peeks out from the student's mouth. I try rescuing him but it turns out to be difficult. The student, each time more anxious, repeats: It's all chicanery. I hear Alberto repeating, from inside of the student, that everything's fine, that we shouldn't worry; he says: It's fine, it's fine. I don't know what's happening, but I get the feeling that everything gets more complicated. This state of confusion lasts a long time and everything gets darker until we're in a bank. Alberto wants to sell a broom; a naked girl attends him. I try making him notice that the girl is naked, but Alberto scowls and motions with his hand. Then I notice that the entire bank is made of old rags and that's why it smells disgusting. I tell Alberto this, but he's very focused on counting the money he gets. And yet, later, instead of money in our pockets, we have cold butter and we're very anxious because we don't want it to melt and ruin our clothes (because, although our appearance is pitiful, we're certain that we're well dressed). Suddenly there's a woman with muslin in her mouth; her singing covers everything in some sort of perfume. The chorus of the eight hundred drinkers that suddenly appears in the background to support her melody has a different effect, converting everything into a tavern.

Alberto and I are in a room in an English university trying to sleep on the floor, but we're covered by blankets that are too small for us. Each time I'm about to fall asleep, an old woman enters the room and adjusts our blankets with a violence that is distorted by her kind face. Alberto also wakes up each time this happens. We try telling her to stop doing this, but she says: Who is going to help you once you're asleep? I see that Alberto is blinking: he's very anxious, and that's because he understands, like I do, that if we fall asleep we will be left in this woman's hands, although she has the tact to avoid this situation, which would put her in quite a predicament, impeding our sleep. Due to this, we try getting up, but can't. Then I don't know what happens and suddenly we're on a bridge. There are eight drinkers on behalf of eight hundred. Then we're in an English university giving a lecture on Bloy; for some reason, the students are old women. The odor we feel is of rags.

The students in the English university ask me very difficult questions; I go about answering all of them. This gives me the feeling of knowing everything that can be asked of me and fills me with joy, but all this is interrupted when an eight-foot-tall student asks: What will you do with your hands when you no longer have a head? Alberto looks at me and, blinking, says: Your head is getting too big. Now, there's a tense situation that lasts a long time without climaxing. Suddenly we find ourselves in a room destroying sculptures, and even though we appear happy, we don't feel any type of joy nor anything like it: we feel that we should be enjoying ourselves and that something is denying us this. I find out that my head is the problem: it stretched upwards to the point that it damaged the ceiling; through the visible hole in the ceiling, a few birds come in and take the sculptures. Alberto is furious. He accuses me of not wanting to have a good time. He tells me: This room was all we had. I tell him that, on the one hand, he's exaggerating and, on the other, all of this is just "chicanery," and even though I feel like an idiot saying this word, I repeat it several times. Alberto tells me that this isn't "chicanery" but rather a "chicane" of mine. I ask him to say this in a different way because I don't understand the word (and I repeat "the word" several times, each time more anxious). Suddenly there's an old woman and she asks: Would it be a mysterious relationship? The old woman holds in her arms a baby with a *distinctly* medieval cow's head.

It's all a bit hazy, because we're in an English university, but simultaneously we aren't in any definable place, although we're certain that we're at war. I'm very anxious; I ask Alberto if the same is happening to him and he tells me yes, and that we're anxious because we have to guard the positions we've won and advance over the enemy's territory. But when we try seeing what positions we've won, we don't see them; and when we try defining the enemy, we can't. We *do* know we're at war, although the only indication is that we're anxious, truly anxious. Alberto, as a result of his nerves, blinks, and I feel my head grow. Anxiety and permanent worry, Alberto tells me; and those nerves, he adds, are war (that, at least to him, seems to be a certainty). Everything remains confusing for a long time until, suddenly, we're in a tavern. There are eight hundred drinkers singing a war song that goes: To war / there's nothing more. These two lines are repeated again and again. And above them the melody of the old woman with muslin in her mouth is heard, but this time it's a tense and discordant melody that makes us even more anxious. Then suddenly we're running through a forest in which the trees are burnt or have fallen down or both. Alberto asks: What are we going to do with our hands? I tell him that I don't know, that he's the one who knows what to do, and in that moment a failure stands in front of us. Although we run, the failure remains standing in front us. The failure tells us: I didn't want it to be this way. Alberto gets very anxious. I grab him by the hood and suddenly we're in an English university talking about Clausewitz and his relationship to Thucydides. The students are fascists and we're so anxious that the lecture is terrible. From the classroom's door, the poor-in-spirit observes us.

Alberto and I are giving a lecture in an English university. The lecture doesn't have a clear subject, although it seems we're trying to address war (it appears to be about a war *that's happening*). First, Alberto says that war is latent, that's to say, present but invisible. Then I add that war isn't the act of war but rather the feeling it produces. The students, the majority of whom are fascists (for some reason we're certain that they are), don't want to understand this. We continue with the subject of war by writing out different variations of a phrase, for example:

– war is to be anxious
– to be at war is to be anxious
– to be anxious is to be at war

And many others like that until we find one which, in that moment, seems perfect to us: war is a state of anxiety. The phrase keeps echoing until one of the students, who is eight feet tall, asks: War is a state of the soul? And an old woman asks: Would it be a mysterious relationship of war? It's then we realize that we should've clarified that war, despite all of this, exists independent of anxiety, but that we didn't to avoid sounding contradictory. Alberto says to me: We should've said the following: The state of anxiety is one way to live war; the other is to participate in it, but for that it's essential to know what to do. I tell him that this sounds good to me, but that I'd add the following: To know what to do is the only way of nullifying anxiety or of transforming anxiety into action. Alberto tells me that this sounds good to him and when we're about to explain all of this to the students, we're suddenly in a forest with trees that are simultaneously burnt and healthy. In the background, there's a beautiful yet tense and discordant melody; that's to say, a melody that's beautiful but not relaxing. And in the background, eight hundred drinkers who repeat: We agree / war is all you see. Meanwhile, although we're not running, we get the feeling that we're running very fast. In the distance, like a desired but not really desired objective (that's to say, an objective that fulfills the role of the desired), we see a failure who is simultaneously a poor-in-spirit. Along the sides, eight hundred old women applaud us.

Alberto greets me from the end of a road that goes downwards. I seem to take a couple of hours in arriving at where he is; when I reach him we're suddenly in an English university talking about things we know nothing about. The students notice that we don't know what we're talking about and stand up: they're all eight feet tall. Together, they grab us and it seems as though the group were only one huge student with dozens of arms, but it's only a feeling because we know that they're a group of students. Suddenly we find ourselves on a ship talking to an old woman. The old woman says we're geniuses, but for some reason it bothers me that she says it like this and I respond that if we were geniuses we wouldn't have anything to decide. In that moment we realize that what we have to do on this ship is teach, so that's what we do. While we're giving the lecture (which doesn't have a subject) we notice that the students don't understand what we're saying and ask questions unrelated to the subject (because even though there's no fixed subject, it feels like there's a subject and what the students say feels different). Everything keeps on like this until a students asks: Which one of you will help me?

The student is two feet tall and looks like a baby. Alberto approaches him and picks him up in his arms and in that moment three things coincide: Alberto is an old woman, I see him mummified, and the baby-student has a *distinctly* medieval cow's head. For some reason, the situation becomes tense; Alberto blinks and that makes me think about war. The image that suddenly appears in that moment is one of a trench full of soldiers.

On an English university's blackboard is written: If we don't do anything, afterwards we'll be able to do everything. This phrase (it's a certainty) was written by militant fascists from an English university. Upon reading the phrase, Alberto and I feel that we're terrorists because we don't know what we're capable of. I ask Alberto: How could we stop being terrorists? Mummified, Alberto responds: One must act and err like Che. And Alberto, now completely mummified and yet still himself, says: Che wasn't a terrorist because he knew what to do, that's to say, he used his intelligence to make it so the possibilities that the world offered him were not so many; like that, little by little, the possibilities were each time fewer until he only had one; few people achieve this, although it happens to many, like, for example, the terminally ill, who at one moment, towards the end, are only left with dying; or babies, who can only grow; in reality, it happens to everyone: the only difference is to have or not have been able to have made one or many decisions, that's to say, to have acted after thinking or simultaneously, or, in any case, that one has deliberately searched for that situation at which one arrives. And yet, in that moment,

I realize that in order to act this way, it would be necessary to abandon the state of anxiety that is war; Alberto, as if he were listening, tells me: War, as long as it is a state of anxiety, immobilizes, and that immobilization turns us all into terrorists. And, in that moment, he repeats: One must act and err like Che. But all this unproductive productivity dissolves when we're suddenly on a ship giving a lecture to a group of very old students who, when we don't establish any relationships because we don't know what we're saying, ask us things like: Would it be a mysterious relationship? Then we're in an airport and see approaching us three girls who are returning from a nightclub and are sweaty from dancing so much; the girls move towards us, but the moment is censored (although we feel anxiety); the censorship makes everything dark and it stays like this until one of them asks us for a relationship between Bloy and Lawrence of Arabia. Alberto looks at me and says that he doesn't know; I don't know anything either and in that moment we notice that the girls are old and very drunk. Afterwards we're suddenly in an English university giving a lecture but there aren't any students (except for an old woman who, instead of listening, sings a beautiful melody that dissolves all problems).

26

Alberto is about to finish building something that looks blurry although we know that it's a machine that yields something positive. I have the same machine in front of me and, so it seems, I've already finished building it. Then there's a few minutes of confusion until, without anything happening in the middle, the machines we've built start attacking us. Now it's clear what they are: they have the shape of an eight-foot-tall student and the smell of an old rag. Alberto tells me: We made things that destroy us. I tell Alberto that what he's saying is obvious, although that doesn't mean, I tell him, that it ceases to be true. Alberto keeps talking to me and at some point in the conversation (which seems to be only noise, because I can't make sense of what he's saying), the dangerous situation we're experiencing dissolves and we're suddenly on a ship. Alberto talks about the *enigma of the earlier situation* and it's clear that by "earlier situation" he's not referring to what happened to us *earlier*. I ask, then, what he's referring to, but he says that he can't know; he tells me: I can't solve the enigma because it is an enigma; if I were to solve it, it would cease to be an enigma and then we wouldn't be able to think about it and I like thinking about it. In that moment, I'm certain that, in reality, Alberto can't think about the enigma precisely because he likes the enigma; then what he doesn't like is thinking about the enigma, because thinking about the enigma supposes to attempt to undo it. I want to tell him my conclusion but something impedes me; I gather my strength and when I'm about to do it, a poor-in-spirit is suddenly there and *he* tells him. I see that Alberto is fascinated by this discovery and this fascination seems to tint everything white. Suddenly we're in an English university giving a lecture to two students: one failure and a poor-in-spirit. The lecture is about something that isn't clearly understood but which has to do with the annoyance of having to think against oneself. The subject, I'm certain, was decided by the poor-in-spirit; Alberto tells me: He wants to know about what he doesn't know. I respond yes, that's why one teaches, and he responds: Yes, but he knows that he will never know about that. In that moment, we're suddenly on a ship and Alberto wants to jump off. He wants to reach an island in the distance. I tell him that the island is far away, but he tells me: If we get there, we get there. So we jump, but upon falling we're suddenly in an English university giving a lecture on random topics.

27

We're on a ship and, in the distance, an island to which Alberto wants to go can be seen. He tells me: Everything's on that island. Suddenly, we notice that the ship, which is simultaneously a bridge, is full of dead, fat people; Alberto tells me: They died, *but* because of an obesity problem. A little surprised, I ask him what he means with the "but." Alberto, a little annoyed, scowls and motions for me to keep quiet because he's very focused on staring at the island and repeating "everything's there." Alberto wants to jump into the water, but I come up with a better idea; I tell him: If the ship is simultaneously a bridge, then it can take us to the island. But this situation disappears and suddenly we're in a restroom in an English university, which is simultaneously the restroom of a nightclub and simultaneously the kitchen of a church (we find this triple situation a certainty). Alberto wants to go out to the street, but something stops us. An old woman is making a steaming soup; when we approach her to take a look inside the cauldron, there's suddenly some type of censorship which makes us think about an old rag. A very tall student tells us: The problem is that the rag is knitted: half of the things can't be seen. And as if the student's words were something to be fulfilled, suddenly we see only half of the things that are there. Alberto tells me: Everything's there but only half of it's visible. The argument that builds up between Alberto and me, on one side, and the students of an English university, on the other, is as follows: how can one know that what one sees is half of something, that's to say, that it's not simply something complete with the appearance of half of something? Alberto and I want to believe that the half is hidden but, somehow, available; the students say that they're appearances of halves that, in reality, are complete things and not halves. The conclusion at which we arrive is as follows: be they halves of something or complete things, the fact that they're presented as halves makes the other half claim existence. This conclusion fills us with happiness. Everything that follows has a party-like atmosphere that's interrupted when we notice that the students are still arguing over the non-visible half's type of existence.

The ship-island situation is repeated; Alberto says: Everything's there. He wants to jump off but I suggest we use the ship as a bridge. We're discussing this when suddenly we're in an English university giving a lecture. But neither Alberto nor I want to give the lecture so we talk about random things: about him, about me, about what we had for breakfast, about the things we don't like. The students are deeply interested and are participating so much that they don't let us talk. Like that we manage to escape, because they remain discussing pants and stop paying attention to us. Somehow, we're able to control the following moment and suddenly we're on the ship. Now very determined, Alberto wants to jump off the ship, but I insist on using the ship as a bridge and arriving at the island *properly*. In that moment, Alberto throws himself into the water and I don't know whether to follow him or not. My hesitation is so great that it gives me an unpleasant feeling. Suddenly we're in an English university talking about Lawrence of Arabia, but everything we're capable of saying is so basic that even the students know more than we do. Intermittently, there's suddenly the ship scene and the previous incident repeats itself: Alberto jumps off and I hesitate over whether I should jump off as well. Then, all that's left is the censored hesitation.

We find ourselves with a student who wants to tell us something; we tell him to go ahead but he hesitates; a lot of time passes until he feels encouraged and says: War is the chicanery of being anxious. In that moment, Alberto and I feel that this phrase is our fault. Then we're in a tavern with eight hundred drinkers who toast looking at us: it's a toast in our honor. One of them stands up and, winking at us, shouts: We're terrorists because we don't know what to do. Hurried, we go out to a black courtyard and we're suddenly on a ship that is simultaneously a bridge. Everything's black except an island seen in the distance. Alberto tells me: That island is twenty yards away. I tell him that it's at least a mile away, but he insists it's very close. He wants to jump off and swim to the island, but I propose something else: Let's use the ship, which is also a bridge. Alberto doesn't want to wait and says he's going to swim to the island. He jumps into the water and I don't know whether I should follow him or not. Then suddenly we're in a room destroying sculptures; everything seems to be going well, but, doing this, I don't feel any emotion; and yet I'm certain that such an act could be emotional. Alberto accuses me of not wanting to have a good time. We hear, through the broken roof, an old woman singing with muslin in her mouth; in the background, a chorus of eight hundred drinkers sings: We agree / war is all you see / this terror. The melody of the old woman is beautiful and subdued; it goes: In the distance / there's a space of vagrance / a paradise / for the tired. Above the eight hundred drinkers and the old woman, we see an old man who is a pigeon flying despite having broken wings. Alberto tells me: And yet, he's flying. But the old man looks like he's about to fall at any moment.

30

Alberto and I are on a ship trying to find an old psychic who charges too much. We find her, we talk with her and she tells us: You're both going to an island. We ask how much we owe her and she gives us a price that's lower than expected. We pay and thank her. When we leave, we discover that the old woman with whom we were talking wasn't the one we were looking for, but rather another one who doesn't charge much and has a bad reputation. Suddenly we're on a different ship than the one we were on before. Alberto looks at me and says: We're in an English university. I say that this is impossible although I see a classroom and some students waiting. We don't know whether we should go in or not; Alberto tells me: I don't know what we could come to talk about. When we look closely at the students, we notice that there are eight hundred of them; we look even closer and notice that they're in a tavern and that they're drinkers. I try telling Alberto something but he scowls and motions for me to keep quiet. Suddenly we're in a black room; in front of us there's a baby with a distinctly medieval cow's head; behind him, five sweaty girls. The baby says: Fascists say it's better to not do anything so that afterwards everything can be done; and adds: But I don't say this. The girls shout excitedly and take the baby away and, in that moment, we notice that they are old women.

31

Suddenly we're on a ship and there's an island in the distance. Alberto tells me: It's not so far away. He looks like he's willing to jump. I try convincing him that we should use the ship as a bridge to get to the island, but Alberto tells me that it would take too long. And even though it's impossible to know whether this would or wouldn't take long, I'm certain he's right. Alberto throws himself into the water and I try following him but can't. I say: I can't jump. There is suddenly a poor-in-spirit and he replies: It's fine, that's what it's for. What is? I ask. He says: The book you're reading. I look and see that I have a book in my hand and that I'd never be able to jump with a book in my hand. Suddenly we find ourselves in a black room. The floor moves and Alberto, pointing at something, tells me: The floor is rotten. I look up and see that someone is taking notes on everything we do. He's writing down that the floor is rotten. Behind him, through a hole in the ceiling, we see an old man who is a pigeon flying just fine with completely broken wings. Alberto says: His wings are broken *and yet* he's flying: he doesn't know it but he does it. I ask him to explain why he says "and yet" and why he says "he doesn't know it," but before Alberto responds, we're suddenly sitting on a bench. Alberto removes a hat that he has on and I do the same. When I look at his cap, I notice the name *Alberto* is written on the inside. Mine also has my name, and Alberto says: I feel as if we've known each other since long ago. This comment makes such little sense that everything darkens as if the light were covered by an old rag.

32

Alberto is in the water and I'm on a ship. It looks like Alberto has just jumped off. He tells me: We're going to the island, everything's there. But I can't jump. A poor-in-spirit who's in front of me tells a failure: He has a book in his hand; he won't be able to jump like that. Suddenly there's an old woman and she tells me: Give me that book. I reply that I can't, that I need it. The old woman, very kindly, asks me why. I respond: This is what it's for. But in that moment, surrounded by all of them, I become suspicious of the excessive amount of help. I'm at war, I tell myself: I shouldn't believe anyone. I look down and see Alberto; he's playing and floating on his back. He says to me: Let's go to the island, everything's there. I don't know what to do. Suddenly there's a group of eight-foot-tall students and they want to take the book away, supposedly to help me; suddenly, the image of a room with sculptures appears before me, and as a result of that lesson, I throw the book before they take it away. The ones who helped me, upon seeing me about to jump, try to stop me: they grab me by my head and hands. In that moment, I realize that they couldn't care less about the book. With a lot of effort, I'm able to jump; upon falling, I feel that I'm drowning and this feeling lasts a long time. The scene repeats itself, again and again, the jump and then the drowning, until Alberto and I suddenly find ourselves in a black tavern with eight hundred drinkers singing: War, in the past / was all we had / in this life / we agree / war is all you see. Alberto has a broom in his hand and wants to sell it. He offers it to one of the drinkers; the drinker, still singing, but simultaneously talking to us, says: I like it, I'll buy it. Now Alberto has a stack of bills in his hand and wants to buy a house in the countryside. For some reason, I'm certain such a purchase would end in disaster. I tell Alberto: No, don't buy. Alberto scowls and motions for me to keep quiet, and yet he throws the money on the floor and kicks it. Then we're on a ship and Alberto wants to jump to an island that's in front of us; he tells me: Everything's on that island. I suggest we use the ship like a bridge, but he says no and jumps into the water. I remain above, very relaxed, reading a book.

33

I'm with Alberto and we're on a ship trying to read a book between the two of us, but we can't because there are eight hundred drinkers on the deck drinking wine that smells like old rags and singing: War to me / is terrifying / and that's why I'm anxious. The melody of what they're singing is so lively that Alberto and I join them, although, for some reason, we only pretend to sing: we stand among them and move our mouths. Everything goes on like this until one of them notices that we aren't really singing and shouts: These ones aren't singing. Alberto looks at me and says: It's time to go to the island. What island? I ask. He points in the far distance and says: Everything's there. And without saying anything else, Alberto jumps off the ship. I hesitate: I see Alberto below, in the water, waiting for me, and the drinkers, above, threatening me with their fists although they don't look like they've decided to harm me. This situation lasts a long time until we're suddenly in a black tavern. There are eight hundred drinkers drinking and toasting to us while shouting: We toast to them! We go along with them and together we all start singing something like the following: A terrorist / doubts his own sight /

but I enjoy what I see / because I don't believe / that such a thing even exists. And we continue like this for a long time, feeling very lively.

I'm with Alberto and I don't know what's going on. We're there and not there simultaneously or alternately: when we're there, the place is a ship, although not too clearly, and the ship moves and advances in the opposite direction of an island that Alberto points to while his eyes fill with tears; when we aren't there, it's not clear why, but we feel darkness; and when we're in both places simultaneously, it's a layering without conflict, between being and not being: it's a suspension of everything. In this suspension, Alberto thinks to enter an island that can't be seen. Suddenly we're on an island and for some reason can't open our eyes, although I'm certain that this is the place we've been searching for.

Alberto says so many things so quickly that I don't understand him. I know that he's talking about an island where, so he says, everything can be found. The more time passes, the more I find Alberto confusing. The place we're in seems to be a dark and empty tavern. At one particular moment, I understand Alberto to say: One enters the island through darkness, in suspension. I respond in a serious tone: When I understand, I understand less; I prefer the incomprehensible murmur. Alberto laughs. Flowers fall from the ceiling and, upon hitting the floor, make an unpleasant sound. I grab one (although I feel like I'm grabbing more than a hundred) and smell it: it's rotten. Alberto takes it away from me and uses it to clean his black boots. But the more he cleans them, the dirtier they get. I tell him: Alberto, those boots are disgusting. Suddenly we find ourselves in a bank and Alberto wants to sell the broom in his hand; he says to me: I was thinking of giving it to my nephew, but maybe it's better to sell it and buy new boots. We proceed to a situation in which Alberto has already sold the broom and bought the black boots he's wearing. I look at them and notice one heel is much higher than the other; they're poorly made. I tell

Alberto that he's walking as if he's lame, but he scowls and motions for me to keep quiet. I don't know how, but afterwards we're suddenly on a ship; it's already night and for some reason we're sad. Alberto points to an island in the distance; he tells me: Everything's on that island, right? I tell him yes, but I try to be honest and tell myself that I don't know. Then I tell Alberto that I don't know and he says that he's already realized this.

36

Alberto and I are in an English university, strolling through a park and admiring the architecture; Alberto tells me: Look at that gothic dome. Four very tall students approach us and say: We want to learn from you. We respond that we have nothing to teach, but they insist: We want to hear about Bloy. Somehow, we're suddenly in a tavern and there's an old woman on a stage singing as if she has muslin in her mouth. The song goes: During war / my lullaby will terrify / anyone who smiles for more than two minutes. But the song is of such sweetness that we begin to rise and arrive, no one knows how, at an English university. Three students approach us; they're eight feet tall and look dangerous. Alberto scowls, makes a motion with his hand, and whispers in my ear: They're fascists. We want to escape, but our legs are so heavy and moving is so difficult that we can't and they capture and lift us up in the air. This scene repeats itself again and again (it's not clear how many times, but it has the effect of an obligatory and prolonged repetition): we try escaping, but our legs move with such heaviness that they always capture us. This repetition is distressing above all because there's no reason that we shouldn't be able to escape. Alberto tells me: It's this that we have to fulfill. I respond: The book (I have one in my hand) that I'm reading is for this. And in that moment we're suddenly in a trench full of soldiers singing a terrible song. A soldier approaches us and says: We're all very anxious. Alberto, with a smile, responds: Of course, because we're at war. The soldier remains thinking; after some time he tells us: We're very anxious not because we're at war, but rather we're at war because we're anxious. I intervene and say: No, the two things are the same: war *is* to be anxious. The soldiers stop doing whatever they were doing and start laughing at what I just said, but I don't feel that they're mocking me, but rather that they understand that what I said is a joke. I laugh with them and this moment of communal joy lasts until suddenly Alberto and I are ordering breakfast in a bar. When the waitress arrives with our food, we try looking at her cleavage, but can't see anything because in its depth everything seems to be made of old rags.

37

It's dark, it's raining and there's a cold wind that makes us shiver. Alberto says: I don't complain about that which is strange. And yet, this situation isn't strange: there's wind and rain and we're having a really bad time. This lasts for a while until suddenly there's a poor-in-spirit who tells us: I want to hear you talk about books, I want you to tell me I'm crazy. But we don't know anything, we can't talk about any book. The poor-in-spirit insists: Talk to me about Bloy, of Paul the Apostle, of Paul the Anchorite, the first Christian anchorite, the one who found his path in solitude. We don't know what to tell him and we feel that the rain is melting our bones (this feeling isn't very clear, but it's a feeling like this one). Now we're in a cave, sheltered from the rain that can be heard outside. There is a poor-in-spirit next to us, he says: Talk to me of the beautiful appearance, of the dryness of the cave, of the path that Paul the Anchorite found. But we really don't know who Paul the Anchorite is and respond: The book you're reading is for that. The poor-in-spirit looks at the book he's holding, he reads for a while and, with a perplexed expression, says: I don't complain about that which is strange, but let me clarify: one is from June

29th, the other from January 15th. Perplexed, we stare at him and he adds: I'm referring to the calendar of saints. Then there's an emptiness that lasts until we're suddenly in a classroom in an English university in front of a group of fascists. We're drenched and don't know what to talk about. One of the students raises his hand and asks for an explanation. What do you want to know? I ask. I don't want to know, he says: I only want you to talk about books, for you to tell me that I'm crazy. The situation is so tense that we leave through some type of hole. Suddenly we're in a black and damp tavern. We feel as if we're made of old rags.

38

Alberto looks at me and, pointing at a dark spot, says: I don't know where we should go. I look at the dark spot and see that we have to choose between three paths. Alberto tells me: This is an *excessive* situation. I tell him I agree, that everything could have been made better, that choosing between paths is unfortunate. In any case we hesitate over what to do. Suddenly there's a conformist (we're certain that he's simultaneously a conformist and a poor-in-spirit) who says: The path you have to choose is this one. We look at the one he points out: there is no difference between that path and the other two. We ask him why that path would be more convenient than the others, but only to see what he says, because we don't trust him. He says something incomprehensible and leaves. Alberto says to me: If what he says is incomprehensible, it's because he just said whatever. I agree, but add: In any case, we don't know which path to take. Alberto remains contemplative; after some time like this, he tells me: We have to devise a plan of action. I tell him that we can't, that it would be impossible to devise a plan originating from the objective situation because we don't know its rules. But Alberto argues: Yes, it must be possible, because the system of contents is rational, and we should devise a plan based on that same system. What Alberto says is true, but I argue in order to provoke him: The system of contents doesn't answer to our needs, it follows its own logic, without taking us into account; like this, it's not possible to devise a plan. We stay silent without knowing what to do, and this lasts until we're suddenly in a trench. Alberto is worried because his black boots are getting muddy. A soldier approaches us and, with a bad attitude, says: You see / war is terrifying. Suddenly we find ourselves in a spring and Alberto takes advantage of this to clean his black boots. Then suddenly we're in an auto-repair shop; then in a hair salon; then suddenly back in a trench. Alberto tells me: I'd like to be still for a while. But the movement is inevitable and we keep passing from one place to another until I realize what's happening: we pass so quickly from one place to another that the places start blending into each other. Then we're in a hair salon but there's someone fixing a car and someone else is a muddy soldier in a trench. Everything starts getting worse once there are dead soldiers in the hair salon and sunken cars in the spring and we see that everyone is drinking wine that tastes like rags in the English university. An old woman with muslin in her mouth sings a melody that touches us; it goes: What moves / is a soldier / and by his side / we're all waiting for news / of whether it's possible / to tell us who it is we're waiting for / because a lot of time has passed / and we're more and more tired. In that moment, we remain quiet and realize that we're exhausted. Finally, it's as if we fell asleep, although it's obvious that we're awake.

39

We're in an English university giving a lecture on constellations, but not on constellations that actually exist, but rather on the concept of constellation. Alberto says: We connect these points and the result is ours, but the points were already there. The students don't understand. I insist: The points couldn't have been connected without our intervention and we decide which point to connect with another; because of this, the result, that's to say, the constellation, is a creation of ours built upon something previously present; it can even be said that one *found* a constellation. But the students still don't understand anything. One of them stands up: he's eight feet tall. He wants to ask a question; a little scared, we tell him to go ahead. He tells us: You both talk garbage, you lie, you don't know what you're saying, you treat us like idiots, you think you're ... We're in a spring; Alberto, as he cleans his black boots, says: I feel as though this place is truly pleasant. I tell him that I feel the same way, and to confirm this I bend down and drink a little water. The water is tasty and that makes me hesitate and ask: Why does the water have a flavor, of what? Alberto tastes the water and tells me: It tastes like old rags. I taste it again and tell him he's right. And yet, this time the taste of old rags isn't unpleasant and remains as a background while we pass from one place to another without being able to stop.

40

Alberto and I are strolling across a bridge when a man with empty eye sockets, that's to say, without eyeballs, approaches us. He's blind, says Alberto. The man hears us, gets closer and says: And yet, I see. And starts saying things like: Here three sticks, there an eagle, that over there's green, and so on. But Alberto stops him and says: You talk to me of things that I see, but that doesn't mean you can see; to prove that, speak of things I *can't* see. The man, then, like someone found cheating, makes a hand motion and leaves. Suddenly we find ourselves in an English university that's simultaneously a tavern. There are eight hundred students drinking wine that tastes like rags (not only are we certain that it tastes like that, but, moreover, it smells like it). One of the students stands up and shouts: They came in! But the shout has no effect because we act as if we're alone. The waitress comes to take our order and we try looking at her cleavage, but don't see anything. Alberto tells me: Its depth is made of old rag. I respond yes, but that if it's truly an old rag we should be able to smell it, and since the atmosphere smells like old rags, we'll never know the truth. Alberto, then, feels sorry that we're condemned to perceive everything through smell; he says to me: We're like dogs. I tell him something that neither he nor I understand and so I probably didn't say anything.

We're on a ship. I look to the right and see a cave; Alberto asks: Why don't you look to the left? I do as he says and see an island full of plants and birds. A music that's neither pleasant nor unpleasant radiates from the island. I tell Alberto: That music is very different. Alberto doesn't understand me and I can't explain myself. Then we're in a tavern full of young women drinking wine. Among them, there's an old woman standing on a table singing a melody that moves us deeply. For some reason, the old woman's legs are young and beautiful. I want to point her legs out to Alberto, but can't find him. I inspect the place with my eyes (at least this is what it feels like) and see him: he's by the table in a state of ecstasy before the old woman's legs. The lyrics of the melody are: Someone activates / the motor of this moment / but I feel / that what happens is much too little. Suddenly we're in a forest in which all the trees alternately look like legs and wood, and we're escaping from something that, even though we don't know what it is, we *do* know the effect it can have on us.

We try to give a lecture in an English university, but the only thing we manage to do is repeat: It's that we're fascinated with the quartets by Shost . . . , Shost . . . But we can never remember his name. A student stands up and asks us to explain what is so fascinating about the quartets by Shost . . . We don't know; or we do, because we're certain that we know why they're fascinating, but we can't explain it; and the second certainty is that if we could remember his name we could explain this fascination. The student, impatient, shouts: You aren't professors! In that moment we're suddenly in a very pleasant place, full of plants, with mountains in the background and a stream. Alberto says: This is what is commonly called beautiful scenery. The place is made to be enjoyed, but I don't feel comfortable. I ask Alberto if he feels the same way and he says yes; and adds: It's because this place seems to be made for us, for us to be fine in, but it doesn't take into account what we need. I look at the place closely and think Alberto is right, although I tell him: And yet, it produces happiness to think that someone made this for and because of us. Alberto agrees and admits that our feeling uncomfortable is irrational. Some time passes and Alberto says to me: I feel that we could be destroyed by this scenery. Afterwards, as an irrational consequence of our irrational feelings, we break everything around us so that we don't end up destroyed ourselves. Upon destroying everything, we regret it and don't understand what we did. Alberto tells me: We didn't plan this destruction so we shouldn't even be capable of regret. Then suddenly we're on a ship; in the distance there's an island.

43

I'm with Alberto and we're slumped on a bench in a plaza. We see how an old man who is a pigeon and has completely broken wings flies. Alberto says: And yet, he flies. As if in response to Alberto's words, in that very moment, the old man begins a trajectory towards the floor, and just before he hits it, we're in a toy store discussing Bloy. Alberto tells me: If we talk a lot maybe they'll give us *that* broom. The broom is lovely and shines. It's made of gold, says the naked sales assistant. Alberto responds: I want it for my nephew. In that moment, I realize that Alberto doesn't know that the sales assistant is naked. I try pointing this out but he scowls and motions for me to keep quiet. Then I realize that even though the sales assistant is very pretty, she has old woman legs; and not only this: she's also wearing black boots. Alberto insults her, pointing at the black boots. Then we're suddenly in a trench. A soldier approaches us and says: This is a peaceful place. Then we see that the soldiers have women's legs and that, while they shoot with their arms, they dance with their legs. On a level deeper than the trench, almost in the center, there's an old woman singing a double song: it's good for war and good for dancing. They're two superimposed songs that sound great together, says a soldier who has an old rag in his hand with which he tries, unsuccessfully, to clean the mud walls. The song is divided into two parts; the first goes: Whoever shoots / knows what it's worth; the second part: He who dances / does the rebirth. There is a moment of darkness that lasts until somehow we're suddenly in a spring. I bend down to drink the water and notice that it's tasty because it's putrid.

Alberto keeps repeating that his name is Alfredo, and I accept this as if it were true, without even asking myself why he's trying to convince me of something that's a fact. But perhaps because deep inside I know that his name is a different one (although I accept the new one as if it were the original), I start doubting what Alberto tells me and this feeling of solitude lasts until we're suddenly in a toy store. Alberto (now with his own name) wants to exchange a gold broom for something else, but he doesn't find anything he likes. We make a mess searching for something; after some time, the disarray is such that we can't move. Suddenly we find ourselves in the same place but tidy and we don't feel like touching anything; through a window we see an island, and in the background we hear an old woman (we don't see her but we're certain it's an old woman, although her voice sounds young) singing a song with lyrics composed of three lines that go: If I look but don't touch / everything shines / understand this as advice. The melody of the song is so beautiful that we remain in a very delightful state of suspension (although we can't help feeling that we're about to fall at any moment).

Alberto and I are sitting on a bench in a plaza and we don't know what to do, and although the landscape doesn't include the possibility, we see an island in the distance and feel like being there but don't ask ourselves how it's even possible to see an island from a bench in a plaza. Then Alberto says: That island is there, but it's as if it weren't. Then we're suddenly in a tavern; there are eight hundred drinkers drinking wine that tastes like rags (the taste of rag is a certainty because we smell it in the air). Alberto says: I'd like to tell the drinkers that their wine tastes like rags; I respond: I'd like to use all of this money (we know that we have a lot of money) to buy better wine and give it to the drinkers. We feel like doing a lot of things, but the possibility of doing them wrong keeps us from moving. In the middle of the tavern there's an old woman singing; the melody is terrible, and the lyrics go: Even though almost everything turns out wrong, always / the possibility of coincidentally doing something right / makes it worth the effort to move. Although I already understand, Alberto explains: That old woman says that it doesn't matter what one does because it's beyond our control whether or not something turns out right. I respond: No, it doesn't matter what one does, because one only has to do what one wants to do; there's nothing else that justifies an action; the possibility of something turning out right or wrong is irrelevant to the action itself. So then we decide to do what we want. Alberto stands on a table and sings: Your wine / dear drinkers / tastes like an old rag ... Immediately the atmosphere becomes tense. The drinkers, anxious, look at their wine with disgust. Many of them vomit. I know that now is the time to buy better wine and give it to them, but I can't move because I think that they won't want it, that they won't like it, or that they'll misinterpret my generosity (for example, as contempt). The old woman whispers in my ear: The most likely outcome is that everything turns out wrong, but it can always turn out right, and you mean well. In that moment, I feel full of energy, I see a flag flapping on the door that says Che Guevara, and so I buy wine with the money in my pocket (it's not clear how I do this, but suddenly the purchased wine is at my side) and pass it around. Everything seems to go well, but the drinkers get angry anyway and, even though they like the wine, insult us. The old woman tells me: The catch in all of this is that things turn out wrong but never because of what one suspects. All of a sudden we're on a bench in a plaza talking to an old woman with beautiful legs; the woman puts her head between our heads and her mouth between our ears and says: You can do whatever you want, there's no responsibility or freedom. What I'm certain of in that moment is that one would be truly free if one could predict the effects of one's actions. I tell Alberto this, but he scowls and motions for me to keep quiet.

46

Alberto and I are on a bench in a plaza arguing over whether it's important to do what one wants or if that's irrelevant because, in any case, one can never know where one went wrong, nor how what one does will turn out. Suddenly we find ourselves on a ship; there's an island in the distance, and on the island there are plants and birds. Alberto tells me that he wants to go there, that over there is where everything we need is, and he throws himself into the water. Suddenly we're in a toy store; Alberto talks about a dead person unknown equally by him as well as the sales assistant and myself. According to him, the dead person is a soldier, and if he was a soldier it means, says Alberto, that we're at war, because soldiers die at war. In that moment, the sales assistant tells us: That must be why I've been so anxious. We try explaining to her that it's not that she's anxious because we're at war but rather that war itself is a state of anxiety; but she doesn't understand, perhaps because we aren't convinced of what we say and stutter badly, and so she tells us with a voice that seems to come from somewhere else: If war were *that* I would not have a problem accepting it. And right at that moment we notice that the sales assistant is poor-in-spirit. Afterwards we're in a trench; there we see a soldier in his underwear sing something about the homosexuality of war; it goes: War is about men fighting each other / that's why / war is not serious. We don't understand him and when we ask him to explain, we see that he is an old woman with beautiful legs. In that moment the desire produced by the sight of those legs restricts our free will. The old woman gets on top of a table and the place turns into a sunken tavern, that's to say, an entire tavern, with all of the details, but stuck in a trench (at least that's how the atmosphere feels). The old woman sings: To you, my friends / I'd give what I've got / these legs / that bring me there before things happen / this house / and this way of hugging each other / and if I don't insist / it's because each one of you will die soon. The old woman's last words blacken the atmosphere, although happy giggling can be heard from the soldiers; when the light returns, we can't see anything until we're suddenly in an English university walking and talking between ourselves as the night falls in a way that's a little abrupt and unexpected.

47

I'm with Alberto and we're trying to talk to a man without eyes about our surroundings, although it's very hard to identify the objects. This lasts for a while until we're suddenly in front of a mirror that reflects us in a horrifying way: Alberto is a mummy and my head is growing. In the mirror, we see that there are eight hundred drinkers and an old woman behind us. When we turn around to look at them directly, they're no longer there, but upon looking into the mirror again we notice that they're still there and that our image is now that of us without any deformations. So then Alberto tells me: They're in the mirror and we're just as much here as there. And yet, I hesitate and ask: We're there and here or only here and that's our reflection, as would be normal? Alberto laughs and responds: If they're there and not here it's because that's a place and not only an image. And right at that moment we see an island in the depth of the mirror that isn't on our side. I tell Alberto: We should be able to go to that side. The old woman, from the mirror, responds: You can't, because you two are there and have an image here, and that which is an image to you is real for us, and thus it doesn't make sense for you to be in one place twice; I mean to say that you're both already here, but not in a way that's at all useful to you. Then we're suddenly in a toy store; a naked old woman assists us and asks us what we want. Alberto tells her that he wants to buy something for a nephew of his, and that he's thinking about a broom; he thinks for a while and adds: A gold broom. The old woman tells him that they don't have gold brooms and Alberto, anxious, cleans his black boots. Then we're walking through a forest full of trees; in each tree there are eight hundred drinkers who produce the unbearable smell of old rags, and that smell ruins our stroll.

48

Alberto and I are on on a still ship. A gypsy spreads some cards; we wait until she gives this look like she doesn't know how to read them and says sorry for not being able to tell us anything useful. Suddenly, we're in a toy store in which there are books instead of toys. We read and time passes as though nothing were going to happen. In that moment, Alberto looks at me and says: Marx died in order to avoid finishing *Capital*. I ignore him and we keep reading until, somehow, we're suddenly in a toy store. The sales assistant is naked; Alberto, without paying attention to this, tells her he wants to buy a broom, but then he says that he wants to exchange the broom in his hand. The situation changes every five seconds (there's a clock that marks time), without stopping. The sales assistant, anxious, blinks, and that makes everything turn black (little by little, blink by blink, such that the scenes are darker each time). Afterwards, we're suddenly in a tavern making toasts and singing with eight hundred drinkers, having a great time. Suddenly Alberto looks at me with an impressive expression of lucidity, he gets on top of a table and, when all the drinkers are silent looking at him, shouts: Marx died because he didn't finish *Capital*. First there's a silence; then only applause and shouts from the drinkers. For some reason, they applaud both of us, and in that moment I'm certain that what Alberto says is true in that moment.

49

We're in a park and hear a voice that tells us: That island is there but it's as if it weren't. And yet, Alberto and I don't know what the voice is referring to nor do we see anything that looks like an island. What we do see at our feet is a box full of coconuts. Alberto grabs one and says: Look, this coconut was hacked in the wrong place; that's why it lost all its liquid and is now useless. I grab the coconut, I look at it and see that, indeed, the attempt to remove it from the palm tree was such that the coconut is now dry. And yet, I tell Alberto, to the naked eye, this coconut is identical to all the others. Alberto responds: Yes, but lighter. So then I grab another coconut and notice the difference. Suddenly we find ourselves in a tavern. A drinker looks at us and, intentionally, lets the glass in his hand fall. The glass breaks and an old woman, from another table, tells us: What just happened there is the law of gravity. She lets another glass fall and repeats: This is the law of gravity. She says this with a mocking tone but with an expression of teaching us something. Later, all the drinkers are doing the same and repeating the phrase, which now seems like a prayer: This is the law of gravity, this is the law of gravity … Above this background noise, the old woman sings: The rupture / gives us delight, gives us the cure / gives us the form of the figure / makes us feel emotions / emotions that are pure. The place starts to sink and simultaneously burn down, and so the water boils. Faced with danger, we don't know where to escape to; Alberto says: We have to act under the threat of ruin. And just when he says this, we're suddenly in a cage that looks like a classroom in an English university; then, a seventy-something professor tells us: Man is the animal capable of posing questions and giving answers. Alberto tells me exactly what I was thinking: That's good, he's right. Immediately we're suddenly in a classroom in an English university telling a group of students younger than us the same thing the professor said before. Each time we utter this phrase, the students applaud. This repeats a couple of times, and, although the applause can be heard louder each time, the scene is fainter each time and little by little dissolves.

50

We're in an English university, and even though we have to give a lecture, we don't know what to talk about, nor do we even know whether we should give the lecture or not. We ask the students what to do. There is a long silence that's broken when we call on a student who raises his hand. The student stands up and says: What needs to be done is to put an end to the Third Period. They all start talking simultaneously and arguing over what the student just said, but no one understands what he means. We turn to him and ask him to explain it to us, but he tells us that he doesn't know what he said, that the voice that came out of him wasn't his, and indeed his voice now is very different from the other one. Alberto whispers in my ear: His voice is less firm and less convincing now. We all regret his lack of ability to explain himself, above all due to the suspicion that Alberto and I have that his response could have been the correct one. Another student raises his hand and, without anyone calling on him, says, in an unpleasant voice: What one must do is defend private property. We all stare at him shocked at the incredible and great stupidity of his response and shocked, above all, at the lack of connection between what was asked and what he responded. In the middle of this shock, the student who had spoken before him spits at his hair and this makes the second student leave the classroom crying; but before leaving, from the door, without ceasing to cry, he says: It wasn't I who spoke, that wasn't my voice. And, indeed, his voice is very different now. The astonishment lasts until Alberto raises his hand and, calling upon himself, says: I believe that what is to be done is sufficiently evident, but what should be analyzed before is whether one can decide and if one has to decide or not, because there would be at least two options: either the problem lies in the fact that one can't decide or it lies in wanting to decide when there's no need to decide but rather act; is this understood? I understand him easily, but the students respond that they don't; Alberto continues: I mean to say that perhaps the problem is that one thinks that one has to decide things on occasions in which the decision to make a decision can only result in a problem, that's to say: imagine that you're walking peacefully when, unexpectedly, you arrive at a forking path, and instead of simply following one of the two paths, which are identical, and about which you have no information, you propose to yourself that what you have to do before continuing is make a decision: what happens? A student, who is eight feet tall, says in a very clear voice: I remain still forever. Alberto, satisfied, responds: Exactly, forever, because there's no way of making a decision, and if you were to make one you wouldn't be doing anything different from what you would have done had you followed the path without stopping, with the difference that you would have felt guilty for having decided incorrectly, because, indisputably, a good decision can't be measured by its effect but rather by the decision itself, and if that decision couldn't have been made, whatever you decide will be wrong. A student, impatient, interrupts him: Then what? Alberto responds: So then what one does, almost always, is something that happens to one, not something that one decides, except in cases in which the only possibility is to decide, because in those cases it's possible and obligatory to do so; for example, if at the aforementioned fork, one of the paths were clearly a minefield; although, of course, the problem is knowing how to recognize minefields.

2006

PABLO KATCHADJIAN was born in Buenos Aires in 1977. He is the author of three novels — *What To Do*, *Thanks*, and *Total Freedom* — and a wide array of short stories, poems, and essays. His artistic collaborations include an operatic adaptation of his work alongside the composer Lucas Fagin.

PRISCILLA POSADA is a literary translator from Spanish into English. She lives in New York City.

MICHAL AJVAZ, *The Golden Age.*
The Other City.

PIERRE ALBERT-BIROT, *Grabinoulor.*

YUZ ALESHKOVSKY, *Kangaroo.*

JOE AMATO, *Samuel Taylor's Last Night.*

ANTÓNIO LOBO ANTUNES, *Knowledge of Hell.*
The Splendor of Portugal.

ALAIN ARIAS-MISSON, *Theatre of Incest.*

GABRIELA AVIGUR-ROTEM, *Heatwave and Crazy Birds.*

MIQUEL BAUÇÀ, *The Siege in the Room.*

ANDREI BITOV, *Pushkin House.*

ANDREJ BLATNIK, *You Do Understand.*
Law of Desire.

LOUIS PAUL BOON, *Chapel Road.*
My Little War.
Summer in Termuren.

IGNÁCIO DE LOYOLA BRANDÃO,
Anonymous Celebrity.
Zero.

CHRISTINE BROOKE-ROSE,
Amalgamemnon.

G. CABRERA INFANTE, *Infante's Inferno.*
Three Trapped Tigers.

JULIETA CAMPOS, *The Fear of Losing Eurydice.*

ANNE CARSON, *Eros the Bittersweet.*

ORLY CASTEL-BLOOM, *Dolly City.*

LOUIS-FERDINAND CÉLINE, *North.*
Conversations with Professor Y.
London Bridge.

ERIC CHEVILLARD, *Demolishing Nisard.*
The Author and Me

RENÉ CREVEL, *Putting My Foot in It.*

RALPH CUSACK, *Cadenza.*

NICHOLAS DELBANCO, *Sherbrookes.*
The Count of Concord.

NIGEL DENNIS, *Cards of Identity.*

JEAN ECHENOZ, *Chopin's Move.*

LESLIE A. FIEDLER, *Love and Death in the American Novel.*

ANDY FITCH, *Pop Poetics.*

GUSTAVE FLAUBERT, *Bouvard and Pécuchet.*

MAX FRISCH, *I'm Not Stiller.*
Man in the Holocene.

CARLOS FUENTES, *Christopher Unborn.*
Distant Relations.
Terra Nostra.

TAKEHIKO FUKUNAGA, *Flowers of Grass.*

PAULO EMÍLIO SALES GOMES, *P's Three Women.*

JUAN GOYTISOLO, *Count Julian.*
Juan the Landless.

KEIZO HINO, *Isle of Dreams.*

KAZUSHI HOSAKA, *Plainsong.*

YORAM KANIUK, *Life on Sandpaper.*

ZURAB KARUMIDZE, *Dagny.*

JOHN KELLY, *From Out of the City.*

GEORGE KONRÁD, *The City Builder.*

TADEUSZ KONWICKI, *A Minor Apocalypse.*
The Polish Complex.

ANNA KORDZAIA-SAMADASHVILI,
Me, Margarita.

MENIS KOUMANDAREAS, *Koula.*

ELAINE KRAF, *The Princess of 72nd Street.*

JIM KRUSOE, *Iceland.*

AYSE KULIN, *Farewell: A Mansion in Occupied Istanbul.*

EMILIO LASCANO TEGUI, *On Elegance While Sleeping.*

ERIC LAURRENT, *Do Not Touch.*

VIOLETTE LEDUC, *La Bâtarde.*

MARIO LEVI, *Istanbul Was a Fairy Tale.*

DEBORAH LEVY, *Billy and Girl.*

JOSÉ LEZAMA LIMA, *Paradiso.*

ROSA LIKSOM, *Dark Paradise.*

YURI LOTMAN, *Non-Memoirs.*

HISAKI MATSUURA, *Triangle.*

DONAL MCLAUGHLIN, *beheading the virgin mary, and other stories.*

ABDELWAHAB MEDDEB, *Talismano.*

ESHKOL NEVO, *Homesick.*

WILFRIDO D. NOLLEDO, *But for the Lovers.*

BORIS A. NOVAK, *The Master of Insomnia.*

CLAUDE OLLIER, *The Mise-en-Scène.*
Wert and the Life Without End.

FERNANDO DEL PASO, *News from the Empire.*
Palinuro of Mexico.

ROBERT PINGET, *The Inquisitory.*
Mahu or The Material.
Trio.

RAYMOND QUENEAU, *The Last Days.*
Odile.
Pierrot Mon Ami.
Saint Glinglin.

ANN QUIN, *Berg.*
Passages.
Three.
Tripticks.

JOÃO UBALDO RIBEIRO, *House of the Fortunate Buddhas.*

ALAIN ROBBE-GRILLET, *Project for a Revolution in New York.*
A Sentimental Novel.

ALIX CLEO ROUBAUD, *Alix's Journal.*

JACQUES ROUBAUD, *The Form of a City Changes Faster, Alas, Than the Human Heart.*
The Great Fire of London.
Hortense in Exile.
Hortense Is Abducted.
Mathematics: The Plurality of Worlds of Lewis.

TOMAŽ ŠALAMUN, *Soy Realidad.*

LUIS RAFAEL SÁNCHEZ, *Macho Camacho's Beat.*

STIG SÆTERBAKKEN, *Siamese.*
Self-Control.
Through the Night.

ARNO SCHMIDT, *Collected Novellas.*
Collected Stories.
Nobodaddy's Children.
Two Novels.

MARKO SOSIČ, *Ballerina, Ballerina*

GONÇALO M. TAVARES, *A Man: Klaus Klump.*
Jerusalem.
Learning to Pray in the Age of Technique.

TOR ULVEN, *Replacement.*

MATI UNT, *Brecht at Night.*
Diary of a Blood Donor.
Things in the Night.

ÁLVARO URIBE & OLIVIA SEARS, EDS., *Best of Contemporary Mexican Fiction.*

ELOY URROZ, *Friction.*
The Obstacles.

DOUGLAS WOOLF, *Wall to Wall.*
Ya! & John-Juan.

JAY WRIGHT, *Polynomials and Pollen.*
The Presentable Art of Reading Absence.

PHILIP WYLIE, *Generation of Vipers.*

REYOUNG, *Unbabbling.*

VLADO ŽABOT, *The Succubus.*

ZORAN ŽIVKOVIĆ, *Hidden Camera.*

LOUIS ZUKOFSKY, *Collected Fiction.*

VITOMIL ZUPAN, *Minuet for Guitar.*

SCOTT ZWIREN, *God Head.*

AND MORE . . .